Betsy Everitt

Harcourt Brace Jovanovich, Publishers

San Diego   New York   London

HBJ

Copyright © 1990 by Betsy Everitt

Requests for permission to make copies of any part
of the work should be mailed to: Permissions Department,
Harcourt Brace Jovanovich, Publishers, 8th Floor, Orlando, Florida 32887.

Library of Congress Cataloging-in-Publication Data
Everitt, Betsy.
Frida the wondercat/by Betsy Everitt.
p.   cm.
Summary: Louise and her cat, Frida, find a magical collar
on their doorstep, which changes their lives.
ISBN 0-15-229540-2
ISBN 0-15-229541-0 (pbk.)
[1. Cats—Fiction.   2. Magic—Fiction.]   I. Title.
PZ7.E9217Fr   1990
[E]—dc19   88-30064

A B C D E
A B C D E (pbk.)

The paintings in this book were done in gouache on Bristol
kid finish paper.
The text type was set in Adroit Light by HBJ Photocomposition
Center, San Diego, California.
Printed and bound by South China Printing Co. Ltd., Hong Kong
Production supervision by Warren Wallerstein and Michele Weekes
Designed by Nancy J. Ponichtera

Printed in Hong Kong

For my mom and dad

Louise and her cat, Frida, were best friends.
They did everything together.

One morning they opened the front door.
A mysterious blue box sat on the front step.

It looked like a present, so Louise opened it.
Inside was a beautiful ruffled collar.

Louise tried the collar on, but it was too small.
"It must be for you, Frida," she said.

The collar fit Frida perfectly!
At first it seemed to be an ordinary collar, but the next day . . .

. . . Frida began to do strange things. And in the days
that followed, she became more and more amazing.

She played the piano and wore funny socks.

She cooked bean soup . . .

. . . and went to the post office.

On Sundays, she drove a bus.

Soon Frida was the talk of the town.
Louise was happy to have a wondercat.

She invited the neighbors over for lunch.

The guests were truly amazed when Frida served
her fabulous bean soup and ice-cream pie . . .

. . . and danced a waltz with Simon from next door.

Frida became so famous that people came from miles around to
ride in the bus driven by a cat. She drove them around town . . .

. . . and into the hills. Frida was very, very busy.

But Louise began to miss Frida.

And Frida missed Louise. The collar had changed their lives.

Then one very busy Sunday, Louise had an idea.

Later that night, she whispered it to Frida.

The next day, they put the ruffled collar back into the blue box.

They walked across the grass and tiptoed past the tulips . . .

. . . and quietly left the box at Simon's house.

The next morning, they woke up to a very loud noise.

Louise and Frida looked out the window. Simon's dog was mowing the lawn—and proudly wearing the ruffled collar!

Simon was happy to have a wonderdog.

And Louise and Frida were happy to have each other.